Bliss Carman

Low Tide on Grand Pré

A Book of Lyrics

Bliss Carman

Low Tide on Grand Pré
A Book of Lyrics

ISBN/EAN: 9783744786904

Printed in Europe, USA, Canada, Australia, Japan

Cover: Foto ©Andreas Hilbeck / pixelio.de

More available books at **www.hansebooks.com**

LOW TIDE ON GRAND PRÉ

THE TITLEPAGE IS DESIGNED BY
MR. MARTIN MOWER, AND THE
COVER BY MR. GEORGE H. HALLOWELL

FIRST EDITION,
NOVEMBER 25th, 1893.

SECOND EDITION,
MARCH 15th, 1894.

The text of the first edition of LOW TIDE ON GRAND
PRÉ *is here reproduced without alteration, except for a line in*
"*The Eavesdropper*" *and the addition of* "*Marian Drury,*"
"*Golden Rowan,*" *and* "*A Sea Drift.*"

PREFATORY NOTE TO THE FIRST EDITION

The poems in this volume have been collected with reference to their similarity of tone. They are variations on a single theme, more or less aptly suggested by the title, LOW TIDE ON GRAND PRÉ. *It seemed better to bring together between the same covers only those pieces of work which happened to be in the same key, rather than to publish a larger book of more uncertain aim.*

B. C.

By Grand Pré,
September, 1893.

A TABLE OF THE CONTENTS OF THIS BOOK

S. M. C.

Spiritus haeres sit patriae quae tristia nescit.

LOW TIDE ON GRAND PRÉ

THE sun goes down, and over all
   These barren reaches by the tide
Such unelusive glories fall,
   I almost dream they yet will bide
   Until the coming of the tide.

And yet I know that not for us,
   By any ecstasy of dream,
He lingers to keep luminous
   A little while the grievous stream,
   Which frets, uncomforted of dream—

Low Tide on Grand Pré

A grievous stream, that to and fro
    Athrough the fields of Acadie
Goes wandering, as if to know
    Why one beloved face should be
    So long from home and Acadie.

Was it a year or lives ago
    We took the grasses in our hands,
And caught the summer flying low
    Over the waving meadow lands,
    And held it there between our hands?

The while the river at our feet—
    A drowsy inland meadow stream—
At set of sun the after-heat
    Made running gold, and in the gleam
    We freed our birch upon the stream.

Low Tide on Grand Pré

There down along the elms at dusk
  We lifted dripping blade to drift,
Through twilight scented fine like musk,
  Where night and gloom awhile uplift,
  Nor sunder soul and soul adrift.

And that we took into our hands
  Spirit of life or subtler thing—
Breathed on us there, and loosed the bands
  Of death, and taught us, whispering,
  The secret of some wonder-thing.

Then all your face grew light, and seemed
  To hold the shadow of the sun;
The evening faltered, and I deemed
  That time was ripe, and years had done
  Their wheeling underneath the sun.

Low Tide on Grand Pré

So all desire and all regret,
  And fear and memory, were naught;
One to remember or forget
  The keen delight our hands had caught;
  Morrow and yesterday were naught.

The night has fallen, and the tide . . . .
  Now and again comes drifting home,
Across these aching barrens wide,
  A sigh like driven wind or foam:
  In grief the flood is bursting home.

WHY

FOR a name unknown,
Whose fame unblown
Sleeps in the hills
  For ever and aye;

For her who hears
The stir of the years
Go by on the wind
  By night and day;

Low Tide on Grand Pré

And heeds no thing
Of the needs of spring,
Of autumn's wonder
  Or winter's chill;

For one who sees
The great sun freeze,
As he wanders a-cold
  From hill to hill;

And all her heart
Is a woven part
Of the flurry and drift
  Of whirling snow;

Why

For the sake of two
Sad eyes and true,
And the old, old love
So long ago.

THE UNRETURNING

THE old eternal spring once more
   Comes back the sad eternal way,
With tender rosy light before
   The going-out of day.

The great white moon across my door
   A shadow in the twilight stirs;
But now forever comes no more
   That wondrous look of Hers.

MARIAN DRURY

MARIAN DRURY, Marian Drury,
　　How are the marshes full of the sea!
Acadie dreams of your coming home
　　All year through, and her heart gets free, —

Free on the trail of the wind to travel,
　　Search and course with the roving tide,
All year long where his hands unravel
　　Blossom and berry the marshes hide.

23

Low Tide on Grand Pré

Marian Drury, Marian Drury,
   How are the marshes full of the surge !
April over the Norland now
   Walks in the quiet from verge to verge.

Burying, brimming, the building billows
   Fret the long dikes with uneasy foam.
Drenched with gold weather, the idling willows
   Kiss you a hand from the Norland home.

Marian Drury, Marian Drury,
   How are the marshes full of the sun !
Blomidon waits for your coming home,
   All day long where the white wings run.

Marian Drury

All spring through they falter and follow,
  Wander, and beckon the roving tide,
Wheel and float with the veering swallow,
  Lift you a voice from the blue hillside.

Marian Drury, Marian Drury,
  How are the marshes full of the rain!
April over the Norland now
  Bugles for rapture, and rouses pain, —

Halts before the forsaken dwelling,
  Where in the twilight, too spent to roam,
Love, whom the fingers of death are quelling,
  Cries you a cheer from the Norland home.

Low Tide on Grand Pré

Marian Drury, Marian Drury,
   How are the marshes filled with you!
Grand Pré dreams of your coming home, —·
   Dreams while the rainbirds all night through,

Far in the uplands calling to win you,
   Tease the brown dusk on the marshes wide;
And never the burning heart within you
   Stirs in your sleep by the roving tide.

A WINDFLOWER

BETWEEN the roadside and the wood,
  Between the dawning and the dew,
A tiny flower before the sun,
  Ephemeral in time, I grew.

And there upon the trail of spring,
  Not death nor love nor any name
Known among men in all their lands
  Could blur the wild desire with shame.

Low Tide on Grand Pré

But down my dayspan of the year
 The feet of straying winds came by;
And all my trembling soul was thrilled
 To follow one lost mountain cry.

And then my heart beat once and broke
 To hear the sweeping rain forebode
Some ruin in the April world,
 Between the woodside and the road.

To-night can bring no healing now;
 The calm of yesternight is gone;
Surely the wind is but the wind,
 And I a broken waif thereon.

IN LYRIC SEASON

THE lyric April time is forth
  With lyric mornings, frost and sun;
  From leaguers vast of night undone
Auroral mild new stars are born.

And ever at the year's return,
  Along the valleys gray with rime,
  Thou leadest as of old, where time
Can naught but follow to thy sway.

Low Tide on Grand Pré

The trail is far through leagues of spring,
  And long the quest to the white core
  Of harvest quiet, yet once more
I gird me to the old unrest.

I know I shall not ever meet
  Thy still regard across the year,
  And yet I know thou wilt draw near,
When the last hour of pain and loss

Drifts out to slumber, and the deeps
  Of nightfall feel God's hand unbar
  His lyric April, star by star,
And the lost twilight land reveal.

THE PENSIONERS

WE are the pensioners of Spring,
　And take the largess of her hand
When vassal warder winds unbar
　The wintry portals of her land;

The lonely shadow-girdled winds,
　Her seraph almoners, who keep
This little life in flesh and bone
　With meagre portions of white sleep.

Low Tide on Grand Pré

Then all year through with starveling care
   We go on some fool's idle quest,
And eat her bread and wine in thrall
   To a fool's shame with blind unrest.

Until her April train goes by,
   And then because we are the kin
Of every hill flower on the hill
   We must arise and walk therein.

Because her heart as our own heart,
   Knowing the same wild upward stir,
Beats joyward by eternal laws,
   We must arise and go with her;

The Pensioners

Forget we are not where old joys
    Return when dawns and dreams retire;
Make grief a phantom of regret,
    And fate the henchman of desire;

Divorce unreason from delight;
    Learn how despair is uncontrol,
Failure the shadow of remorse,
    And death a shudder of the soul.

Yea, must we triumph when she leads.
    A little rain before the sun,
A breath of wind on the road's dust,
    The sound of trammeled brooks undone,

Low Tide on Grand Pré

Along red glinting willow stems
  The year's white prime, on bank and stream
The haunting cadence of no song
  And vivid wanderings of dream,

A range of low blue hills, the far
  First whitethroat's ecstasy unfurled:
And we are overlords of change,
  In the glad morning of the world,

Though we should fare as they whose life
  Time takes within his hands to wring
Between the winter and the sea,
  The weary pensioners of Spring.

AT THE VOICE OF A BIRD

Consurgent ad vocem volucris.

CALL to me, thrush,
   When night grows dim,
When dreams unform
   And death is far!

When hoar dews flush
   On dawn's rathe brim,
Wake me to hear
   Thy wildwood charm,

35

Low Tide on Grand Pré

As a lone rush
  Astir in the slim
White stream where sheer
  Blue mornings are.

Stir the keen hush
  On twilight's rim
When my own star
  Is white and clear.

Fly low to brush
  Mine eyelids grim,
Where sleep and storm
  Will set their bar;

At the Voice of a Bird

For God shall crush
  Spring balm for him,
Stark on his bier
  Past fault or harm,

Who once, as flush
  Of day might skim
The dusk, afar
  In sleep shall hear

Thy song's cool rush
  With joy rebrim
The world, and calm
  The deep with cheer.

Low Tide on Grand Pré

Then, Heartsease, hush !
  If sense grow dim,
Desire shall steer
  Us home from far.

WHEN THE GUELDER ROSES BLOOM

When the Guelder roses bloom,
Love, the vagrant, wanders home.

Love, that died so long ago,
As we deemed, in dark and snow,

Comes back to the door again,
Guendolen, Guendolen.

Low Tide on Grand Pré

In his hands a few bright flowers,
Gathered in the earlier hours,

Speedwell-blue, and poppy-red,
Withered in the sun and dead,

With a history to each,
Are more eloquent than speech.

In his eyes the welling tears
Plead against the lapse of years.

When the Guelder Roses Bloom

And that mouth we knew so well,
Hath a pilgrim's tale to tell.

Hear his litany again :
" Guendolen, Guendolen ! "

" No, love, no, thou art a ghost !
Love long since in night was lost.

" Thou art but the shade of him,
For thine eyes are sad and dim."

Low Tide on Grand Pré

" Nay, but they will shine once more,
  Glad and brighter than before,

" If thou bring me but again
  To my mother Guendolen !

" These dark flowers are for thee,
  Gathered by the lonely sea.

" And these singing shells for her
  Who first called me wanderer,

When the Guelder Roses Bloom

" In whose beauty glad I grew,
  When this weary life was new."

  Hear him raving ! " It is I.
  Love once born can never die."

" Thou, poor love, thou art gone mad
  With the hardships thou hast had.

" True, it is the spring of year,
  But thy mother is not here.

"True, the Guelder roses bloom
   As long since about this room,

"Where thy blessed self was born
   In the early golden morn

"But the years are dead, good lack !
   Ah, love, why hast thou come back,

"Pleading at the door again,
   'Guendolen, Guendolen'?"

When the Guelder Roses Bloom

When the Guelder roses bloom,
And the vernal stars resume

Their old purple sweep and range,
I can hear a whisper strange

As the wind gone daft again,
"Guendolen, Guendolen !"

"When the Guelder roses blow,
Love that died so long ago,

Low Tide on Grand Pré

"Why wilt thou return so oft,
With that whisper sad and soft

"On thy pleading lips again,
'Guendolen, Guendolen'!"

Still the Guelder roses bloom,
And the sunlight fills the room,

Where love's shadow at the door
Falls upon the dusty floor.

When the Guelder Roses Bloom

And his eyes are sad and grave
With the tenderness they crave,

Seeing in the broken rhyme
The significance of time,

Wondrous eyes that know not sin
From his brother death, wherein

I can see thy look again,
Guendolen, Guendolen.

Low Tide on Grand Pré

And love with no more to say,
In this lovely world to-day

Where the Guelder roses bloom,
Than the record on a tomb,

Only moves his lips again,
"Guendolen, Guendolen!"

Then he passes up the road
From this dwelling, where he bode

When the Guelder Roses Bloom

In the by-gone years.   And still,
As he mounts the sunset hill

Where the Guelder roses blow
With their drifts of summer snow,

I can hear him, like one dazed
At a phantom he has raised,

Murmur o'er and o'er again,
"Guendolen, Guendolen !"

Low Tide on Grand Pré

And thus every year, I know,
When the Guelder roses blow,

Love will wander by my door,
Till the spring returns no more ;

Till no more I can withstand,
But must rise and take his hand

Through the countries of the night,
Where he walks by his own sight,

When the Guelder Roses Bloom

To the mountains of a dawn
That has never yet come on,

Out of this fair land of doom
Where the Guelder roses bloom,

Till I come to thee again,
Guendolen, Guendolen.

SEVEN THINGS

THE fields of earth are sown
　From the hand of the striding rain,
And kernels of joy are strewn
　Abroad for the harrow of pain.

I.

The first song-sparrow brown
　That wakes the earliest spring,
When time and fear sink down,
　And death is a fabled thing.

Seven Things

II.

The stealing of that first dawn
   Over the rosy brow,
When thy soul said, " World, fare on,
   For Heaven is here and now! "

III.

The crimson shield of the sun
   On the wall of this House of Doom,
With the garb of war undone
   At last in the narrow room.

IV.

A heart that abides to the end,
   As the hills for sureness and peace,
And is neither weary to wend
   Nor reluctant at last of release.

53

Low Tide on Grand Pré

v.

Thy mother's cradle croon
  To haunt thee over the deep,
Out of the land of Boon
  Into the land of Sleep.

vi.

The sound of the sea in storm,
  Hearing its captain cry,
When the wild, white riders form,
  And the Ride to the Dark draws nigh.

vii.

But last and best, the urge
  Of the great world's desire,
Whose being from core to verge
  Only attains to aspire.

A SEA CHILD

THE lover of child Marjory
　　Had one white hour of life brim full;
Now the old nurse, the rocking sea,
　　Hath him to lull.

The daughter of child Marjory
　　Hath in her veins, to beat and run,
The glad indomitable sea,
　　The strong white sun.

PULVIS ET UMBRA

THERE is dust upon my fingers,
    Pale gray dust of beaten wings,
Where a great moth came and settled
    From the night's blown winnowings.

Harvest with her low red planets
    Wheeling over Arrochar ;
And the lonely hopeless calling
    Of the bell-buoy on the bar,

Pulvis et Umbra

Where the sea with her old secret
  Moves in sleep and cannot rest.
From that dark beyond my doorway,
  Silent the unbidden guest

Came and tarried, fearless, gentle,
  Vagrant of the starlit gloom,
One frail waif of beauty fronting
  Immortality and doom ;

Through the chambers of the twilight
  Roaming from the vast outland,
Resting for a thousand heart-beats
  In the hollow of my hand.

" Did the volley of a thrush-song
    Lodge among some leaves and dew
Hillward, then across the gloaming
    This dark mottled thing was you ?

" Or is my mute guest whose coming
    So unheralded befell
From the border wilds of dreamland,
    Only whimsy Ariel,

" Gleaning with the wind, in furrows
    Lonelier than dawn to reap,
Dust and shadow and forgetting,
    Frost and reverie and sleep ?

Pulvis et Umbra

" In the hush when Cleopatra
    Felt the darkness reel and cease,
Was thy soul a wan blue lotus
    Laid upon her lips for peace ?

" And through all the years that wayward
    Passion in one mortal breath,
Making thee a thing of silence,
    Made thee as the lords of death ?

" Or did goblin men contrive thee
    In the forges of the hills
Out of thistle-drift and sundown
    Lost amid their tawny rills,

Low Tide on Grand Pré

" Every atom on their anvil
     Beaten fine and bolted home,
   Every quiver wrought to cadence
     From the rapture of a gnome ?

" Then the lonely mountain wood-wind,
     Straying up from dale to dale,
   Gave thee spirit, free forever,
     Thou immortal and so frail !

" Surely thou art not that sun-bright
     Psyche, hoar with age, and hurled
   On the northern shore of Lethe,
     To this wan Auroral world !

Pulvis et Umbra

" Ghost of Psyche, uncompanioned,
    Are the yester-years all done ?
Have the oars of Charon ferried
    All thy playmates from the sun ?

" In thy wings the beat and breathing
    Of the wind of life abides,
And the night whose sea-gray cohorts
    Swing the stars up with the tides.

.

" Did they once make sail and wander
    Through the trembling harvest sky,
Where the silent Northern streamers
    Change and rest not till they die ?

Low Tide on Grand Pré

" Or from clouds that tent and people
   The blue firmamental waste,
 Did they learn the noiseless secret
   Of eternity's unhaste?

" Where learned they to rove and loiter,
   By the margin of what sea?
 Was it with outworn Demeter,
   Searching for Persephone?

" Or did that girl-queen behold thee
   In the fields of moveless air?
 Did these wings which break no whisper
   Brush the poppies in her hair?

Pulvis et Umbra

" Is it thence they wear the pulvil—
　　Ash of ruined days and sleep,
　And the two great orbs of splendid
　　Melting sable deep on deep !

" Pilot of the shadow people,
　　Steering whither by what star
　Hast thou come to hapless port here,
　　Thou gray ghost of Arrochar ?"

For man walks the world with mourning
　　Down to death, and leaves no trace,
　With the dust upon his forehead,
　　And the shadow in his face.

Low Tide on Grand Pré

Pillared dust and fleeing shadow
  As the roadside wind goes by,
And the fourscore years that vanish
  In the twinkling of an eye.

Beauty, the fine frosty trace-work
  Of some breath upon the pane ;
Spirit, the keen wintry moonlight
  Flashed thereon to fade again.

Beauty, the white clouds a-building
  When God said and it was done ;
Spirit, the sheer brooding rapture
  Where no mid-day brooks no sun.

Pulvis et Umbra

So.   And here, the open casement
  Where my fellow-mate goes free ;
Eastward, the untrodden star-road
  And the long wind on the sea.

What's to hinder but I follow
  This my gypsy guide afar,
When the bugle rouses slumber
  Sounding taps on Arrochar ?

" Where, my brother, wends the by-way,
  To what bourne beneath what sun,
Thou and I are set to travel
  Till the shifting dream be done ?

Low Tide on Grand Pré

" Comrade of the dusk, forever
　　I pursue the endless way
　Of the dust and shadow kindred,
　　Thou art perfect for a day.

" Yet from beauty marred and broken,
　　Joy and memory and tears,
　I shall crush the clearer honey
　　In the harvest of the years.

" Thou art faultless as a flower
　　Wrought of sun and wind and snow,
　I survive the fault and failure.
　　The wise Fates will have it so.

Pulvis et Umbra

" For man walks the world in twilight,
But the morn shall wipe all trace
Of the dust from off his forehead,
And the shadow from his face.

" Cheer thee on, my tidings-bearer !
All the valor of the North
Mounts as soul from flesh escaping
Through the night, and bids thee forth.

" Go, and when thou hast discovered
Her whose dark eyes match thy wings,
Bid that lyric heart beat lighter
For the joy thy beauty brings."

Low Tide on Grand Pré

Then I leaned far out and lifted
　My light guest up, and bade speed
On the trail where no one tarries
　That wayfarer few will heed.

Pale gray dust upon my fingers ;
　And from this my cabined room
The white soul of eager message
　Racing seaward in the gloom.

Far off shore, the sweet low calling
　Of the bell-buoy on the bar,
Warning night of dawn and ruin
　Lonelily on Arrochar.

GOLDEN ROWAN

SHE lived where the mountains go down to the sea,
    And river and tide confer.
      Golden Rowan, in Menalowan,
    Was the name they gave to her.

She had the soul no circumstance
    Can hurry or defer.
      Golden Rowan, of Menalowan,
    How time stood still for her !

Low Tide on Grand Pré

Her playmates for their lovers grew,
    But that shy wanderer,
        Golden Rowan, of Menalowan,
    Knew love was not for her.

Hers was the love of wilding things;
    To hear a squirrel chir
        In the golden rowan, of Menalowan,
    Was joy enough for her.

She sleeps on the hill with the lonely sun,
    Where in the days that were,
        The golden rowan, of Menalowan,
    So often shadowed her.

Golden Rowan

The scarlet fruit will come to fill,
   The scarlet spring to stir
     The golden rowan, of Menalowan,
And wake no dream for her.

Only the wind is over her grave,
   For mourner and comforter ;
     And "Golden Rowan, of Menalowan,"
Is all we know of her.

THROUGH THE TWILIGHT

THE red vines bar my window way;
    The Autumn sleeps beside his fire,
For he has sent this fleet-foot day
A year's march back to bring to me
    One face whose smile is my desire,
        Its light my star.

Surely you will come near and speak,
    This calm of death from the day to sever !
And so I shall draw down your cheek
Close to my face—So close !—and know
    God's hand between our hands forever
        Will set no bar.

Low Tide on Grand Pré

Before the dusk falls—even now
  I know your step along the gravel,
And catch your quiet poise of brow,
And wait so long till you turn the latch!
  Is the way so hard you had to travel?
    Is the land so far?

The dark has shut your eyes from mine,
  But in this hush of brooding weather
A gleam on twilight's gathering line
Has riven the barriers of dream :
  Soul of my soul, we are together
    As the angels are !

CARNATIONS IN WINTER

Your carmine flakes of bloom to-night
   The fire of wintry sunsets hold ;
Again in dreams you burn to light
   A far Canadian garden old.

The blue north summer over it
   Is bland with long ethereal days ;
The gleaming martins wheel and flit
   Where breaks your sun down orient ways.

Low Tide on Grand Pré

There, when the gradual twilight falls,
    Through quietudes of dusk afar,
Hermit antiphonal hermit calls
    From hills below the first pale star.

Then in your passionate love's foredoom
    Once more your spirit stirs the air,
And you are lifted through the gloom
    To warm the coils of her dark hair.

A SEA-DRIFT

As the seaweed swims the sea
   In the ruin after storm,
Sunburnt memories of thee
   Through the twilight float and form.

And desire, when thou art gone,
   Roves his desolate domain,
As the meadow-birds at dawn
   Haunt the spaces of the rain.

A NORTHERN VIGIL

HERE by the gray north sea,
   In the wintry heart of the wild,
Comes the old dream of thee,
   Guendolen, mistress and child.

The heart of the forest grieves
   In the drift against my door;
A voice is under the eaves,
   A footfall on the floor.

77

Low Tide on Grand Pré

Threshold, mirror and hall,
   Vacant and strangely aware,
Wait for their soul's recall
   With the dumb expectant air.

Here when the smouldering west
   Burns down into the sea,
I take no heed of rest
   And keep the watch for thee.

I sit by the fire and hear
   The restless wind go by,
On the long dirge and drear,
   Under the low bleak sky.

A Northern Vigil

When day puts out to sea
  And night makes in for land,
There is no lock for thee,
  Each door awaits thy hand !

When night goes over the hill
  And dawn comes down the dale,
It's O for the wild sweet will
  That shall no more prevail !

When the zenith moon is round,
  And snow-wraiths gather and run,
And there is set no bound
  To love beneath the sun,

Low Tide on Grand Pré

O wayward will, come near
  The old mad willful way,
The soft mouth at my ear
  With words too sweet to say !

Come, for the night is cold,
  The ghostly moonlight fills
Hollow and rift and fold
  Of the eerie Ardise hills !

The windows of my room
  Are dark with bitter frost,
The stillness aches with doom
  Of something loved and lost.

A Northern Vigil

Outside, the great blue star
  Burns in the ghostland pale,
Where giant Algebar
  Holds on the endless trail.

Come, for the years are long,
  And silence keeps the door,
Where shapes with the shadows throng
  The firelit chamber floor.

Come, for thy kiss was warm,
  With the red embers' glare
Across thy folding arm
  And dark tumultuous hair!

Low Tide on Grand Pré

And though thy coming rouse
    The sleep-cry of no bird,
The keepers of the house
    Shall tremble at thy word.

Come, for the soul is free !
    In all the vast dreamland
There is no lock for thee,
    Each door awaits thy hand.

Ah, not in dreams at all,
    Fleering, perishing, dim,
But thy old self, supple and tall,
    Mistress and child of whim !

A Northern Vigil

The proud imperious guise,
　　Impetuous and serene,
The sad mysterious eyes,
　　And dignity of mien !

　　　　.

Yea, wilt thou not return,
　　When the late hill-winds veer,
And the bright hill-flowers burn
　　With the reviving year ?

When April comes, and the sea
　　Sparkles as if it smiled,
Will they restore to me
　　My dark Love, empress and child ?

Low Tide on Grand Pré

The curtains seem to part;
   A sound is on the stair,
As if at the last . . . I start;
   Only the wind is there.

Lo, now far on the hills
   The crimson fumes uncurled,
Where the caldron mantles and spills
   Another dawn on the world !

THE EAVESDROPPER

In a still room at hush of dawn,
  My Love and I lay side by side
And heard the roaming forest wind
  Stir in the paling autumn-tide.

I watched her earth-brown eyes grow glad
  Because the round day was so fair;
While memories of reluctant night
  Lurked in the blue dusk of her hair.

85

Low Tide on Grand Pré

Outside, a yellow maple tree,
 Shifting upon the silvery blue
With tiny multitudinous sound,
 Rustled to let the sunlight through.

The livelong day the elvish leaves
 Danced with their shadows on the floor;
And the lost children of the wind
 Went straying homeward by our door.

And all the swarthy afternoon
 We watched the great deliberate sun
Walk through the crimsoned hazy world,
 Counting his hilltops one by one.

The Eavesdropper

Then as the purple twilight came
  And touched the vines along our eaves,
Another Shadow stood without
  And gloomed the dancing of the leaves.

The silence fell on my Love's lips;
  Her great brown eyes were veiled and sad
With pondering some maze of dream,
  Though all the splendid year was glad.

Restless and vague as a gray wind
  Her heart had grown, she knew not why.
But hurrying to the open door,
  Against the verge of western sky

Low Tide on Grand Pré

I saw retreating on the hills,
  Looming and sinister and black,
The stealthy figure swift and huge
  Of One who strode and looked not back.

IN APPLE TIME

The apple harvest days are here,
   The boding apple harvest days,
   And down the flaming valley ways,
The foresters of time draw near.

Through leagues of bloom I went with Spring,
   To call you on the slopes of morn,
   Where in imperious song is borne
The wild heart of the goldenwing.

89

Low Tide on Grand Pré

I roamed through alien summer lands,
  I sought your beauty near and far;
  To-day, where russet shadows are,
I hold your face between my hands.

On runnels dark by slopes of fern,
  The hazy undern sleeps in sun.
  Remembrance and desire, undone,
From old regret to dreams return.

The apple harvest time is here,
  The tender apple harvest time;
  A sheltering calm, unknown at prime,
Settles upon the brooding year.

WANDERER

I

WANDERER, wanderer, whither away?
What saith the morning unto thee?
"Wanderer, wanderer, hither, come hither,
Into the eld of the East with me!"

Saith the wide wind of the low red morning,
Making in from the gray rough sea.
"Wanderer, come, of the footfall weary,
And heavy at heart as the sad-heart sea.

Low Tide on Grand Pré

" For long ago, when the world was making,
  I walked through Eden with God for guide;
And since that time in my heart forever
  His calm and wisdom and peace abide.

" I am thy spirit and thy familiar,
  Child of the teeming earth's unrest!
Before God's joy upon gloom begot thee,
  I had hungered and searched and ended the quest.

" I sit by the roadside wells of knowledge;
  I haunt the streams of the springs of thought;
But because my voice is the voice of silence,
  The heart within thee regardeth not.

Wanderer

"Yet I await thee, assured, unimpatient,
　Till thy small tumult of striving be past.
How long, O wanderer, wilt thou a-weary,
　Keep thee afar from my arms at the last?"

II

Wanderer, wanderer, whither away?
　What saith the high noon unto thee?
"Wanderer, wanderer, hither, turn hither,
　Far to the burning South with me,"

Saith the soft wind on the high June headland,
　Sheering up from the summer sea,
"While the implacable warder, Oblivion,
　Sleeps on the marge of a foamless sea!

Low Tide on Grand Pré

" Come where the urge of desire availeth,
    And no fear follows the children of men;
  For a handful of dust is the only heirloom
    The morrow bequeaths to its morrow again.

" Touch and feel how the flesh is perfect
    Beyond the compass of dream to be!
' Bone of my bone,' said God to Adam;
  ' Core of my core,' say I to thee.

" Look and see how the form is goodly
    Beyond the reach of desire and art!
  For he who fashioned the world so easily
    Laughed in his sleeve as he walked apart.

Wanderer

" Therefore, O wanderer, cease from desiring;
    Take the wide province of seaway and sun!
Here for the infinite quench of thy craving,
    Infinite yearning and bliss are one."

III

Wanderer, wanderer, whither away?
What saith the evening unto thee?
" Wanderer, wanderer, hither, haste hither,
    Into the glad-heart West with me!"

Saith the strong wind of the gold-green twilight,
    Gathering out of the autumn hills,
" I am the word of the world's first dreamer
    Who woke when Freedom walked on the hills.

Low Tide on Grand Pré

" And the secret triumph from daring to doing,
 From musing to marble, I will be,
Till the last fine fleck of the world is finished,
 And Freedom shall walk alone by the sea.

" Who is thy heart's lord, who is thy hero?
 Bruce or Cæsar or Charlemagne,
Hannibal, Olaf, Alaric, Roland?
 Dare as they dared and the deed's done again!

" Here where they come of the habit immortal,
 By the open road to the land of the Name,
Splendor and homage and wealth await thee
 Of builded cities and bruited fame.

Wanderer

" Let loose the conquering toiler within thee;
    Know the large rapture of deeds begun!
The joy of the hand that hews for beauty
    Is the dearest solace beneath the sun."

IV

Wanderer, wanderer, whither away?
    What saith the midnight unto thee?
·' Wanderer, wanderer, hither turn home,
    Back to thy North at last to me!"

Saith the great forest wind and lonely,
    Out of the stars and the wintry hills.
" Weary, bethink thee of rest, and remember
    Thy waiting auroral Ardise hills!

Low Tide on Grand Pré

" Was it not I, when thy mother bore thee
In the sweet, solemn April night,
Took thee safe in my arms to fondle,
Filled thy dream with the old delight?

" Told thee tales of more marvelous summers
Of the far away and the long ago,
Made thee my own nurse-child forever
In the tender dear dark land of the snow?

" Have I not rocked thee, have I not lulled thee,
Crooned thee in forest, and cradled in foam,
Then with a smile from the hearthstone of child-
hood
Bade thee farewell when thy heart bade thee
roam?

Wanderer

" Ah, my wide-wanderer, thou blessed vagrant,
Dear will thy footfall be nearing my door.
How the glad tears will give vent at thy coming,
Wayward or sad-heart to wander no more!"

v

Morning and midday I wander, and evening,
April and harvest and golden fall;
Seaway or hillward, taut sheet or saddle-bow,
Only the night wind brings solace at all.

Then when the tide of all being and beauty
Ebbs to the utmost before the first dawn,
Comes the still voice of the morrow revealing
Inscrutable valorous hope—and is gone.

Low Tide on Grand Pré

Therefore is joy more than sorrow, foreseeing
  The lust of the mind and the lure of the eye
And the pride of the hand have their hour of
    triumph,
  But the dream of the heart will endure by-and-by.

AFOOT

THERE'S a garden in the South
  Where the early violets come,
Where they strew the floor of April
  With their purple, bloom by bloom.

There the tender peach-trees blow,
  Pink against the red brick wall,
And the hand of twilight hushes
  The rain-children's least footfall,

Low Tide on Grand Pré

Till at midnight I can hear
    The dark Mother croon and lean
Close above me. And her whisper
    Bids the vagabonds convene.

Then the glad and wayward heart
    Dreams a dream it must obey ;
And the wanderer within me
    Stirs a foot and will not stay.

I would journey far and wide
    Through the provinces of spring,
Where the gorgeous white azaleas
    Hear the sultry yorlin sing.

Afoot

I would wander all the hills
  Where my fellow-vagrants wend,
Following the trails of shadows
  To the country where they end.

Well I know the gypsy kin,
  Roving foot and restless hand,
And the eyes in dark elusion
  Dreaming down the summer land.

On the frontier of desire
  I will drink the last regret,
And then forth beyond the morrow
  Where I may but half forget.

Low Tide on Grand Pré

So another year shall pass,
   Till some noon the gardener Sun
Wanders forth to lay his finger
   On the peach-buds one by one.

And the Mother there once more
   Will rewhisper her dark word,
That my brothers all may wonder,
   Hearing then as once I heard.

There will come the whitethroat's cry,
   That far lonely silver strain,
Piercing, like a sweet desire,
   The seclusion of the rain.

Afoot

And though I be far away,
   When the early violets come
Smiling at the door with April,
   Say, " The vagabonds are home ! "

WAYFARING

Across the harbor's tangled yards
　　We watch the flaring sunset fail;
Then the forever questing stars
　　File down along the vanished trail,

To no discovered country, where
　　They will forgather when the hands
Of the strong Fates shall take away
　　Their burdens and unloose their bands.

Wayfaring

Westward and lone the hill-road gray
    Mounts to the skyline sheer and wan,
Where many a weary dream puts forth
    To strike the trail where they are gone.

The sleepless guide to that outland
    Is the great Mother of us all,
Whose molded dust and dew we are
    With the blown flowers by the wall.

Girt with the twilight she is grave,
    The strong companion, wise and free ;
She leads beyond the dales of time,
    The earldom of the calling sea—

Low Tide on Grand Pré

Beyond these dull green miles of dike,
　And gleaming breakers on the bar—
To the white kingdom of her lord,
　The nameless Word, whose breath we are.

And all the world is but a scheme
　Of busy children in the street,
A play they follow and forget
　On summer evenings, pale with heat.

The dusty courtyard flags and walls
　Are like a prison gate of stone,
To every spirit for whose breath
　The long sweet hill-winds once have blown.

Wayfaring

But waiting in the fields for them
  I see the ancient Mother stand,
With the old courage of her smile,
  The patience of her sunbrown hand.

They heed her not, until there comes
  A breath of sleep upon their eyes,
A drift of dust upon their face ;
  Then in the closing dusk they rise,

And turn them to the empty doors ;
  But she within whose hands alone
The days are gathered up as fruit,
  Doth habit not in brick and stone.

Low Tide on Grand Pré

But where the wild shy things abide,
  Along the woodside and the wheat,
Is her abiding, deep withdrawn ;
  And there, the footing of her feet.

There is no common fame of her
  Upon the corners, yet some word
Of her most secret heritage
  Her lovers from her lips have heard.

Her daisies sprang where Chaucer went ;
  Her darkling nightingales with spring
Possessed the soul of Keats for song ;
  And Shelley heard her skylark sing ;

Wayfaring

With reverent clear uplifted heart
    Wordsworth beheld her daffodils ;
And he became too great for haste,
    Who watched the warm green Cumner hills.

She gave the apples of her eyes
    For the delight of him who knew,
With all the wisdom of a child,
    " A bank whereon the wild thyme grew."

Still the old secret shifts, and waits
    The last interpreter ; it fills
The autumn song no ear hath heard
    Upon the dreaming Ardise hills.

Low Tide on Grand Pré

The poplars babble over it
  When waking winds of dawn go by ;
It fills her rivers like a voice,
  And leads her wanderers till they die.

She knows the morning ways whereon
  The windflowers and the wind confer ;
Surely there is not any fear
  Upon the farthest trail with her !

And yet, what ails the fir-dark slopes,
  That all night long the whippoorwills
Cry their insatiable cry
  Across the sleeping Ardise hills ?

Wayfaring

Is it that no fair mortal thing,
  Blown leaf, nor song, nor friend can stray
Beyond the bourne and bring one word
  Back the irremeable way ?

The noise is hushed within the street ;
  The summer twilight gathers down ;
The elms are still ; the moonlit spires
  Track their long shadows through the town.

With looming willows and gray dusk
  The open hillward road is pale,
And the great stars are white and few
  Above the lonely Ardise trail.

Low Tide on Grand Pré

And with no haste nor any fear,
  We are as children going home
Along the marshes where the wind
  Sleeps in the cradle of the foam.

THE END OF THE TRAIL

ONCE more the hunters of the dusk
　　Are forth to search the moorlands wide,
Among the autumn-colored hills,
　　And wander by the shifting tide.

All day along the haze-hung verge
　　They scour upon a fleeing trace,
Between the red sun and the sea,
　　Where haunts the vision of your face.

115

Low Tide on Grand Pré

The plane at Martock lies and drinks
   The long Septembral gaze of blue;
The royal leisure of the hills
   Hath wayward reveries of you.

Far rovers of the ancient dream
   Have all their will of musing hours:
Your eyes were gray-deep as the sea,
   Your hands lay open in the flowers!

From mining Rawdon to Pereau,
   For all the gold they delve and share,
The goblins of the Ardise hills
   Can horde no treasure like your hair.

The End of the Trail

The swirling tide, the lonely gulls,
  The sweet low wood-winds that rejoice—
No sound nor echo of the sea
  But hath tradition of your voice.

The crimson leaves, the yellow fruit,
  The basking woodlands mile on mile—
No gleam in all the russet hills
  But wears the solace of your smile.

A thousand cattle rove and feed
  On the great marshes in the sun,
And wonder at the restless sea;
  But I am glad the year is done,

Low Tide on Grand Pré

Because I am a wanderer
  Upon the roads of endless quest,
Between the hill-wind and the hills,
  Along the margin men call rest.

Because there lies upon my lips
  A whisper of the wind at morn,
A murmur of the rolling sea
  Cradling the land where I was born;

Because its sleepless tides and storms
  Are in my heart for memory
And music, and its gray-green hills
  Run white to bear me company;

The End of the Trail

Because in that sad time of year,
  With April twilight on the earth
And journeying rain upon the sea,
  With the shy windflowers was my birth;

Because I was a tiny boy
  Among the thrushes of the wood,
And all the rivers in the hills
  Were playmates of my solitude;

Because the holy winter night
  Was for my chamber, deep among
The dark pine forests by the sea,
  With woven red auroras hung,

Low Tide on Grand Pré

Silent with frost and floored with snow,
  With what dream folk to people it
And bring their stories from the hills,
  When all the splendid stars were lit;

Therefore I house me not with kin,
  But journey as the sun goes forth,
By stream and wood and marsh and sea,
  Through dying summers of the North;

Until, some hazy autumn day,
  With yellow evening in the skies
And rime upon the tawny hills,
  The far blue signal smoke shall rise,

The End of the Trail

To tell my scouting foresters
   Have heard the clarions of rest
Bugling, along the outer sea,
   The end of failure and of quest.

Then all the piping Nixie folk,
   Where lonesome meadow winds are low,
Through all the valleys in the hills
   Their river reeds shall blow and blow,

To lead me like a joy, as when
   The shining April flowers return,
Back to a footpath by the sea
   With scarlet hip and ruined fern.

Low Tide on Grand Pré

For I must gain, ere the long night
   Bury its travelers deep with snow,
That trail among the Ardise hills
   Where first I found you years ago.

I shall not fail, for I am strong,
   And Time is very old, they say,
And somewhere by the quiet sea
   Makes no refusal to delay.

There will I get me home, and there
   Lift up your face in my brown hand,
With all the rosy rusted hills
   About the heart of that dear land.

THE VAGABONDS

" Such as wake on the night and sleep on the day, and haunt customable taverns and alehouses and routs about, and no man wot from whence they came, nor whither they go."—*Old English Statute.*

WE are the vagabonds of time,
    And rove the yellow autumn days,
When all the roads are gray with rime
    And all the valleys blue with haze.

We came unlooked for as the wind
    Trooping across the April hills,
When the brown waking earth had dreams
    Of summer in the Wander Kills.

123

Low Tide on Grand Pré

How far afield we joyed to fare,
　　With June in every blade and tree !
Now with the sea-wind in our hair
　　We turn our faces to the sea.

We go unheeded as the stream
　　That wanders by the hill-wood side,
Till the great marshes take his hand
　　And lead him to the roving tide.

The roving tide, the sleeping hills,
　　These are the borders of that zone
Where they may fare as fancy wills
　　Whom wisdom smiles and calls her own.

The Vagabonds

It is a country of the sun,
  Full of forgotten yesterdays,
When time takes Summer in his care,
  And fills the distance of her gaze.

It stretches from the open sea
  To the blue mountains and beyond;
The world is Vagabondia
  To him who is a vagabond.

In the beginning God made man
  Out of the wandering dust, men say;
And in the end his life shall be
  A wandering wind and blown away.

Low Tide on Grand Pré

We are the vagabonds of time,
　Willing to let the world go by,
With joy supreme, with heart sublime,
　And valor in the kindling eye.

We have forgotten where we slept,
　And guess not where we sleep to-night,
Whether among the lonely hills
　In the pale streamers' ghostly light

We shall lie down and hear the frost
　Walk in the dead leaves restlessly,
Or somewhere on the iron coast
　Learn the oblivion of the sea.

The Vagabonds

It matters not.   And yet I dream
  Of dreams fulfilled and rest somewhere
Before this restless heart is stilled
  And all its fancies blown to air.

Had I my will! . . . The sun burns down
  And something plucks my garment's hem;
The robins in their faded brown
  Would lure me to the south with them.

'Tis time for vagabonds to make
  The nearest inn.   Far on I hear
The voices of the Northern hills
  Gather the vagrants of the year.

Low Tide on Grand Pré

Brave heart, my soul ! Let longings bĕ !
We have another day to wend.
For dark or waylay what care we
    Who have the lords of time to friend ?

And if we tarry or make haste,
    The wayside sleep can hold no fear.
Shall fate unpoise, or whim perturb,
    The calm-begirt in dawn austere ?

There is a tavern, I have heard,
    Not far, and frugal, kept by One
Who knows the children of the Word,
    And welcomes each when day is done.

The Vagabonds

Some say the house is lonely set
  In Northern night, and snowdrifts keep
The silent door; the hearth is cold,
  And all my fellows gone to sleep. . . .

Had I my will!   I hear the sea
  Thunder a welcome on the shore;
I know where lies the hostelry
  And who should open me the door.

WHITHER

WHAT shall we do, dearie,
  Dreaming such dreams?
Will they come true, dearie?
  Never, it seems.

Leave the wise thrush alone;
  He knows such things.
How rich the silences
  Fall when he sings!

130

Whither

When shall we come, dearie,
   Into that land
Once was our home, dearie,
   Perfect as planned?

When the wind calling us,
   Some summer day,
Into the long ago
   Lures us away.

Where shall we go, dearie,
   Wandering thus?
Far to and fro, dearie,
   Life leads for us.

Low Tide on Grand Pré

Thou with the morrow's sun
Hillward and free,
I to the vast and hoar
Lone of the sea.

1886–1893.

*And with this the Book of Lyrics,
called Low Tide on Grand Pré, ends.
The Printing is done at the
University Press in Cambridge
for Stone and Kimball.*